MW01107199

Animals in My Backyard
ARMADILLOS

Aaron Carr

LET'S READ
AV²
BY WEIGL™
ADDED VALUE • AUDIO VISUAL

Go to **www.av2books.com**, and enter this book's unique code.

BOOK CODE

L283687

AV² by Weigl brings you media enhanced books that support active learning.

AV² provides enriched content that supplements and complements this book. Weigl's AV² books strive to create inspired learning and engage young minds in a total learning experience.

Your AV² Media Enhanced books come alive with...

Audio
Listen to sections of the book read aloud.

Video
Watch informative video clips.

Embedded Weblinks
Gain additional information for research.

Try This!
Complete activities and hands-on experiments.

Key Words
Study vocabulary, and complete a matching word activity.

Quizzes
Test your knowledge.

Slide Show
View images and captions, and prepare a presentation.

... and much, much more!

Published by AV² by Weigl.
350 5ᵗʰ Avenue, 59ᵗʰ Floor New York, NY 10118
Websites: www.av2books.com www.weigl.com

Library of Congress Cataloging-in-Publication Data
Carr, Aaron.
 Armadillos / Aaron Carr.
     pages cm
 Includes index.
 ISBN 978-1-4896-2930-2 (hard cover : alk. paper) -- ISBN 978-1-4896-2931-9 (soft cover : alk. paper) -- ISBN 978-1-4896-2932-6 (single user ebook)
-- ISBN 978-1-4896-2933-3 (multi-user ebook)
1. Armadillos--Juvenile literature. I. Title.
 QL737.E23C37 2014
 599.3'12--dc23
                            2014039092

Printed in the United States of America in Brainerd, Minnesota
1 2 3 4 5 6 7 8 9 0 18 17 16 15 14

122014
WEP051214

Project Coordinator: Heather Kissock   Designer: Mandy Christiansen

Weigl acknowledges Getty Images, MInden Pictures, and iStock as the primary image suppliers for this title.

Animals in My Backyard
ARMADILLOS

CONTENTS

Meet the armadillo.

She is a small animal with a
hard shell that covers her body.

She lives with her mother when she is young.

When she is young, her shell is soft and gray.

7

Her hard shell is made up of different parts.

The different parts help her move around and curl into a ball.

She has long claws.

Long claws help her
to dig her home.

She drinks water with her long tongue.

With her long tongue,
she can catch insects.

She can smell things
that are under ground.

Under ground, she finds insects and small animals to eat.

She often moves around in the dark of night.

In the dark of night, her long hairs let her know where things are.

17

She lives in North America and South America.

In North America and South America, she can be found in grasslands, forests, and wetlands.

If you meet the armadillo,
she may be afraid.
She might run away.

If you meet the armadillo,
stay away.

ARMADILLO FACTS

These pages provide more detail about the interesting facts found in the book. They are intended to be used by adults as a learning support to help young readers round out their knowledge of each animal featured in the *Animals in My Backyard* series.

Pages 4–5

Armadillos are a family of small- to medium-sized armored mammals. The name armadillo means "little armored one" in Spanish. There are 20 armadillo species, ranging from the 5-inch (12-centimeter) pink fairy armadillo to the 5-foot (1.5-meter) giant armadillo. The only species found in the United States is the nine-banded armadillo. It measures about 2.5 feet (75 cm) long.

Pages 6–7

Armadillos live with their mothers when they are young. Depending on the species, armadillos may give birth to between 1 and 12 babies, called pups. The pups are born with soft, gray shells that take a few days to harden. The mother nurses her pups for two to four months. The pups are mature by the time they are one year old.

Pages 8–9

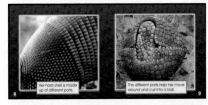

Armadillos have banded shells. Most armadillos have two main sections of shell covering the front and back of the body. These are joined by overlapping bands of shell in the middle. The shell is covered in thousands of scales that are made from the same material as fingernails. The three-banded armadillo of Brazil is the only species that can roll itself into a ball for protection.

Pages 10–11

Armadillos have long, sharp claws. Armadillos use their claws primarily for digging burrows in the ground. They do this both to search for food and to dig shelters for themselves. When threatened by a predator, many armadillo species use their sharp claws to quickly bury themselves in the ground.

Pages 12–13

Armadillos have long tongues. They use their long, sticky tongues to catch insects such as ants and termites. Insects make up the largest part of the armadillo's diet. However, they will also eat small animals, such as small reptiles and amphibians. They have also been known to eat plants on occasion.

Pages 14–15

Armadillos have a strong sense of smell. Since armadillos have poor eyesight, they rely on their sense of smell to help them find food. Using only their strong sense of smell and their excellent digging skills, armadillos are able to track down and capture insects hiding more than 7 inches (18 cm) underground.

Pages 16–17

Armadillos have long hairs that help them find their way in the dark. Although most armadillo species appear mostly hairless at first glance, they usually have long, wiry hairs under their shells. These hairs hang down and drag along the ground. They rub against anything the armadillo may walk over or near, helping the armadillo to feel its way in the dark.

Pages 18–19

Armadillos live in North and South America. The nine-banded armadillo ranges from the American southeast to as far north as Illinois and Nebraska. Armadillos prefer warm climates with suitable grasslands, wetlands, scrub, or forests to serve as their habitat. They burrow into grass, logs, and the ground to make their homes.

Pages 20–21

Armadillos often come in contact with people. For the most part, armadillos do not pose a threat. They largely ignore people unless they feel threatened. People should not attempt to handle armadillos. Their sharp claws could cause harm. Armadillos may also be carriers of a disease called leprosy. However, transmitting this disease to humans is extremely rare.

KEY WORDS

Research has shown that as much as 65 percent of all written material published in English is made up of 300 words. These 300 words cannot be taught using pictures or learned by sounding them out. They must be recognized by sight. This book contains 49 common sight words to help young readers improve their reading fluency and comprehension. This book also teaches young readers several important content words. These words are paired with pictures to aid in learning and improve understanding.

Page	Sight Words First Appearance
4	the
5	a, animal, hard, her, is, she, small, that, with
6	and, lives, mother, when, young
8	different, made, of, parts, up
9	around, help, into, move
10	has, long
11	home, to
12	water
13	can
14	are, things, under
15	eat, finds
16	in, know, let, night, often, where
19	be, found
20	away, if, may, might, run, you

Page	Content Words First Appearance
4	armadillo
5	body, shell
9	ball
10	claws
12	tongue
13	insects
14	ground
16	dark, hairs
18	North America, South America
19	forests, grasslands, wetlands

Check out www.av2books.com for activities, videos, audio clips, and more!

1 Go to www.av2books.com.

2 Enter book code. L 2 8 3 6 8 7

3 Fuel your imagination online!

www.av2books.com